FOX TROT

By Corinne and Jozef Czarnecki

Publishers • GROSSET & DUNLAP • New York

A member of The Putnam Publishing Group

For Claudette and Stella

One brisk autumn morning, Fox was awakened by the familiar sound of huntsmen on horseback. They were following their hounds on the trail of . . . you-know-who.

Fox gulped. "This calls for some fancy footwork."

Quick as a fox, he ran to a nearby riverbank. Paddling swiftly across to the other side, he left the barking hounds behind.

But Fox was not safe yet.

"How on earth can I cross this busy highway?" he yelped. The road most certainly meant hard luck for Fox!

Fox decided to take a different route. Unfortunately, it was the wrong one.

"Grrr!" growled the farmer, gripping his gun. He sounded so angry that even his sheep were scared!

All day poor Fox was chased around the countryside. At last night fell, and not a moment too soon. Fox was exhausted.

"Where are you going to hide?" asked Rabbit.

"The only place that looks safe is the old village church," replied Fox.

Off he ran, faster than you could say "Tally-ho!" To his delight he found a fox-sized window open in the church hall.

"Hmmm...this should do," thought Fox.

With a hop, a skip, and a tired jump,
Fox balanced on the windowsill, knowing
he was safe at last.

"Phew," sighed Fox. "This may not be the coziest den, but at least it's warm and dry."

What Fox didn't know was that he had curled up with the items for tomorrow morning's rummage sale.

Being an early bird, Lucy Trot was
one of the first to arrive at the church hall.
Having an eye for a bargain, she scooped
up Fox before he had time to blink.

"Just what I've always wanted," said
Lucy Trot. "This will keep my neck warm
in winter."

Thrilled with her prize buy, Lucy Trot couldn't wait to get home and try it on.

"Yikes!" thought Fox. "What on earth have I gotten myself into?"

Fox decided the only way out was to wriggle through the biggest hole in Lucy Trot's shopping bag.

"My goodness!" said Lucy. "This bag seems to be coming to life."

Suddenly the bag split open. Lucy gasped with surprise.

"You're a *real* fox!" declared Lucy. "To think I bought you to wear around my neck!"

Fox could see that Lucy was a kind old lady. Quickly he jumped onto her shoulders.

"I don't mind keeping you warm," he said, "if you'll look after me."

So Lucy Trot decided to take Fox home with her.

"We're home, Fox Trot," said Lucy as she opened the gate to her cottage.

"Oh, boy," thought Fox. "With a home like this and a name like that, it's enough to make me want to dance!"

Lucy Trot, who was a rather fussy old lady, decided that what Fox needed first was a good bath.

She scrubbed him with sandalwood soap, dusted him with lavender talc, and finally squirted him with rose-petal perfume.

"Not even the sharpest-nosed hound could trail me now," thought Fox.

That very afternoon, Lucy took Fox to meet her friends. He didn't have the best table manners, but after all was said and done, Fox was far too beautiful and far too precious for Lucy Trot to really mind him eating her cake—even though it was her favorite.

Back home, it wasn't long before they were both ready for bed.

"Good night, Fox Trot!" said Lucy with a sleepy sigh.

"Good night!" said Fox, as he curled up to dream of the treats that awaited him tomorrow.